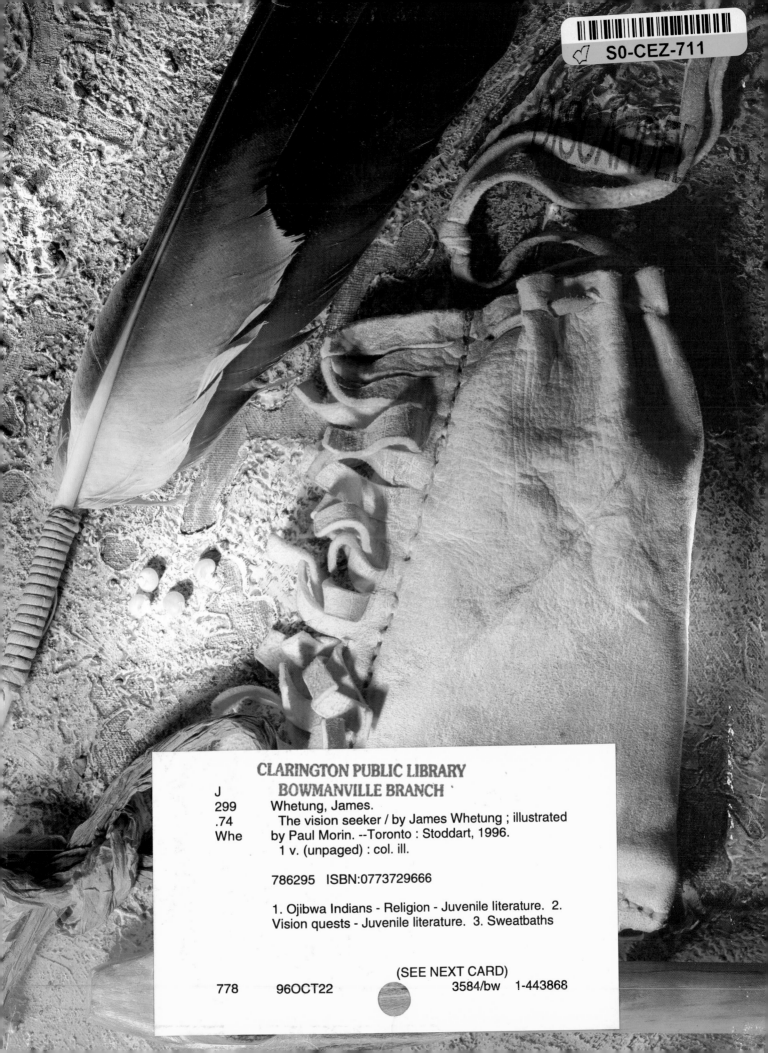

# the VISION SEEKER

## By James Whetung
## Illustrated by Paul Morin

*To all people who are tracing their umbilical cord
to its origins, the Earth Mother.*
        *J.W.*


*To James Whetung,
a helpful guide along my path.*
        *P.M.*

Text copyright © 1996 by James Whetung
Illustrations copyright © 1996 by Paul Morin
Photography by Yusuf Freeman
Book design by Paul Morin

*Stoddart Publishing gratefully acknowledges the support
of the Canada Council, Ontario Ministry of Citizenship,
Culture and Recreation, Ontario Arts Council, and Ontario
Publishing Centre in the development of writing and
publishing in Canada.*

First published in 1996 by
Stoddart Publishing Co. Limited
34 Lesmill Road
Toronto, Canada M3B 2T6, (416) 445-3333

**Canadian Cataloguing in Publication Data**

**Whetung, James**
    **Vision seeker**

**ISBN 0-7737-2966-6**

**1. Ojibwa Indians — Religion — Juvenile literature.
2. Vision quests — Juvenile literature. 3. Sweatbaths
— Juvenile literature. I. Morin, Paul, 1959–    .
II. Title.**

**E99.C6W44 1996    j299'.75    C96-930184-7**

Printed in Hong Kong

**Boozhoo. Greetings, original people.**

**My spirit name is Spirit Bird. My mother's clan is, of common knowledge, Otter. My father says his clan is Black Duck; others say it is Cormorant.**

**We are continuing our celebration of Anishinaabe life as we gather outside this Sweat Lodge. I will guide you through the teaching of how the Anishinaabek people received the original Sweat Lodge.**

Long ago, there was a period of great darkness. Families feuded within families. Neighbors disagreed with neighbors. Whole communities were in conflict. Entire nations fought with each other.

Everywhere men used their pipes and drums for war, for gaining more land. As I said, it was a very dark time.

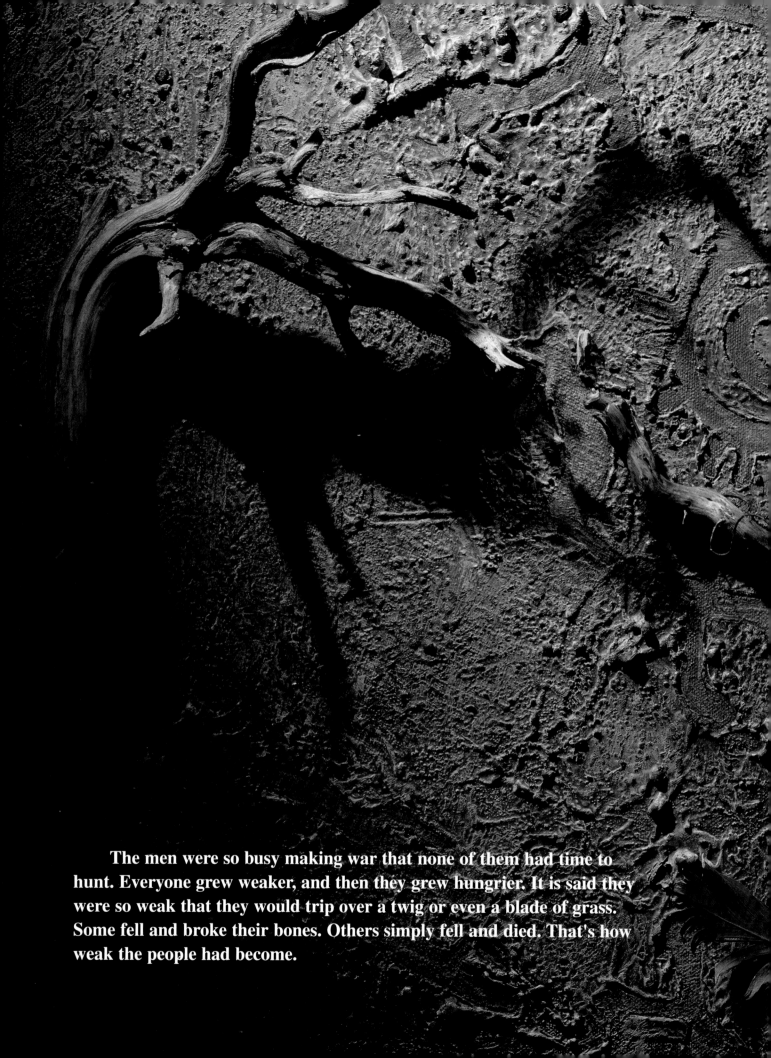

The men were so busy making war that none of them had time to hunt. Everyone grew weaker, and then they grew hungrier. It is said they were so weak that they would trip over a twig or even a blade of grass. Some fell and broke their bones. Others simply fell and died. That's how weak the people had become.

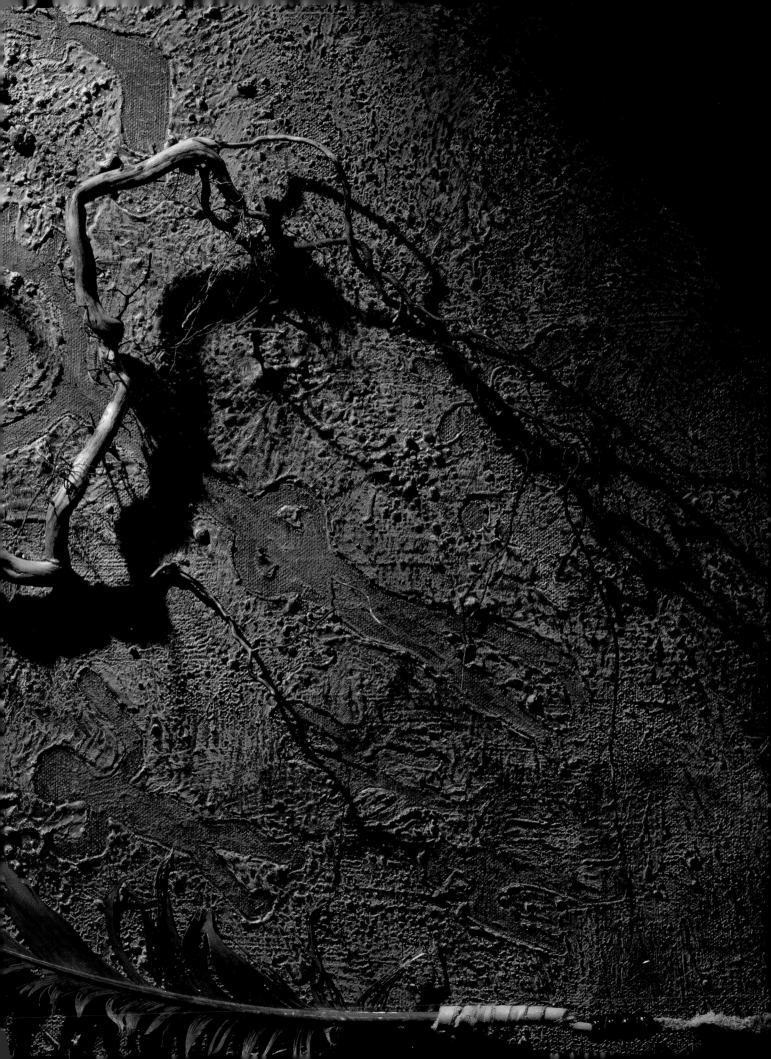

A Little Boy, anxious to help his people, asked his parents what he could do. They told him he could go, go to the high place and seek a vision. Maybe through his fast and the Vision Quest he would learn how to help his people.

The Boy's family helped him to get ready. When he was prepared, his grandmothers, his grandfathers, his aunties and uncles, his mother and father, his brothers and sisters — all of them gathered together to wish the Boy well.

Before he left, his mother and father gave him four kernels of corn.

At sunrise on the first day, the Boy began to walk as far as he could to the East. When the sun set, he knew that he had reached his resting place. So he stopped and ate the first kernel of corn.

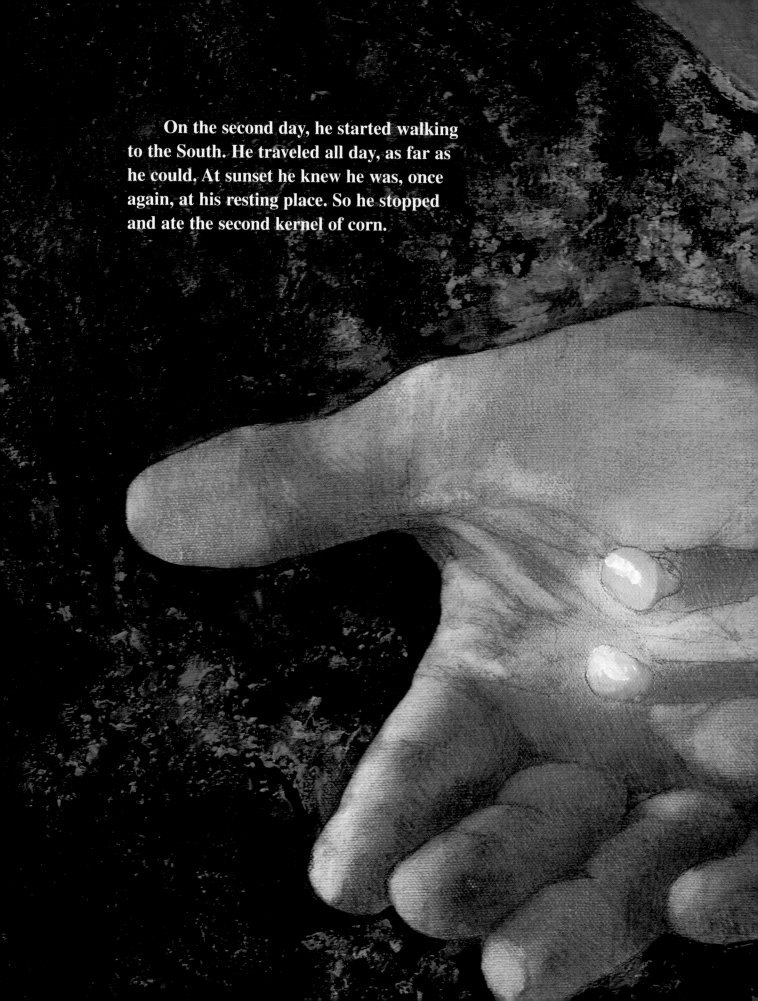

On the second day, he started walking to the South. He traveled all day, as far as he could. At sunset he knew he was, once again, at his resting place. So he stopped and ate the second kernel of corn.

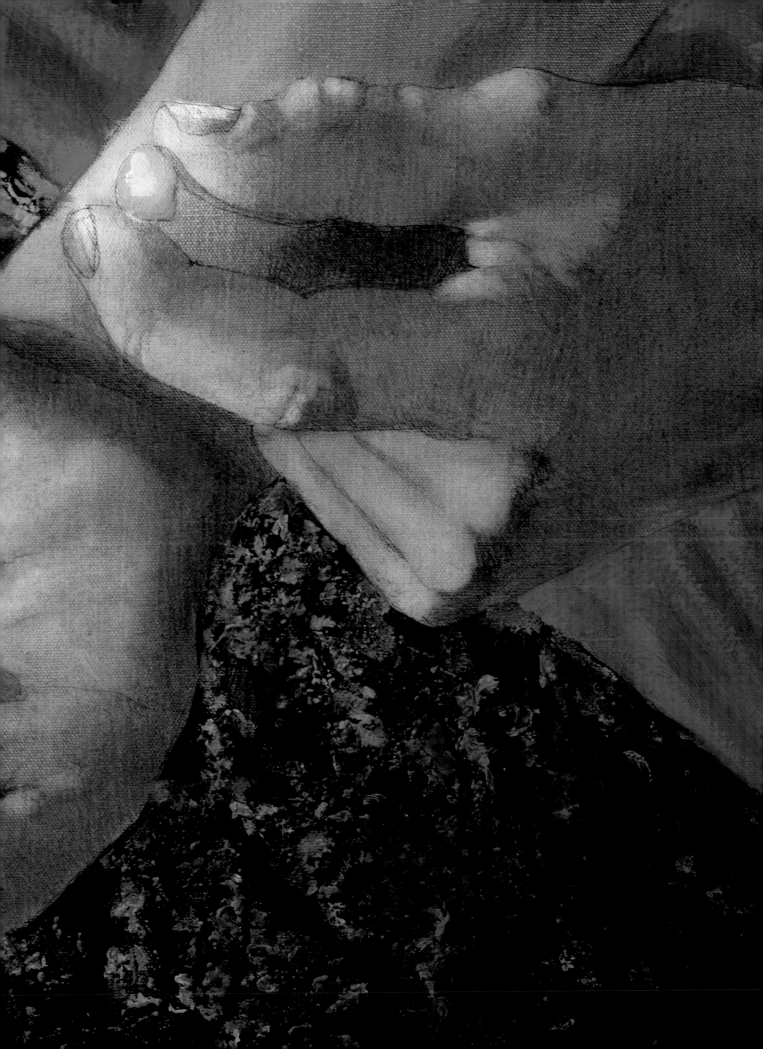

The next day was the third day, and the Boy set out at dawn once
more. He walked all that long day to the West. And once again, when

On the fourth day, the Boy rose at sunrise and walked North until sundown. Finally, he ate the fourth, last kernel of corn.

The Boy had reached the high place, the place where he would seek his vision. And so he rested and began to fast. It is not known how long he went without food and water, but by and by, the Boy began to dream.

In one of his dreams, he traveled through the four levels of color, to the dark side of the moon. When he arrived, he saw a lodge, and inside the lodge he could hear voices. The Little Boy was afraid and shy. But then, a friendly voice called from within.

*"So, you are the Vision Seeker. Come inside, you are welcome. There is nothing to fear."*
The Little Boy stepped forward and entered the lodge.

Inside there were Seven Grandfathers with long, flowing, white hair.
Each and every one of those Grandfathers wore his hair in a different
manner.

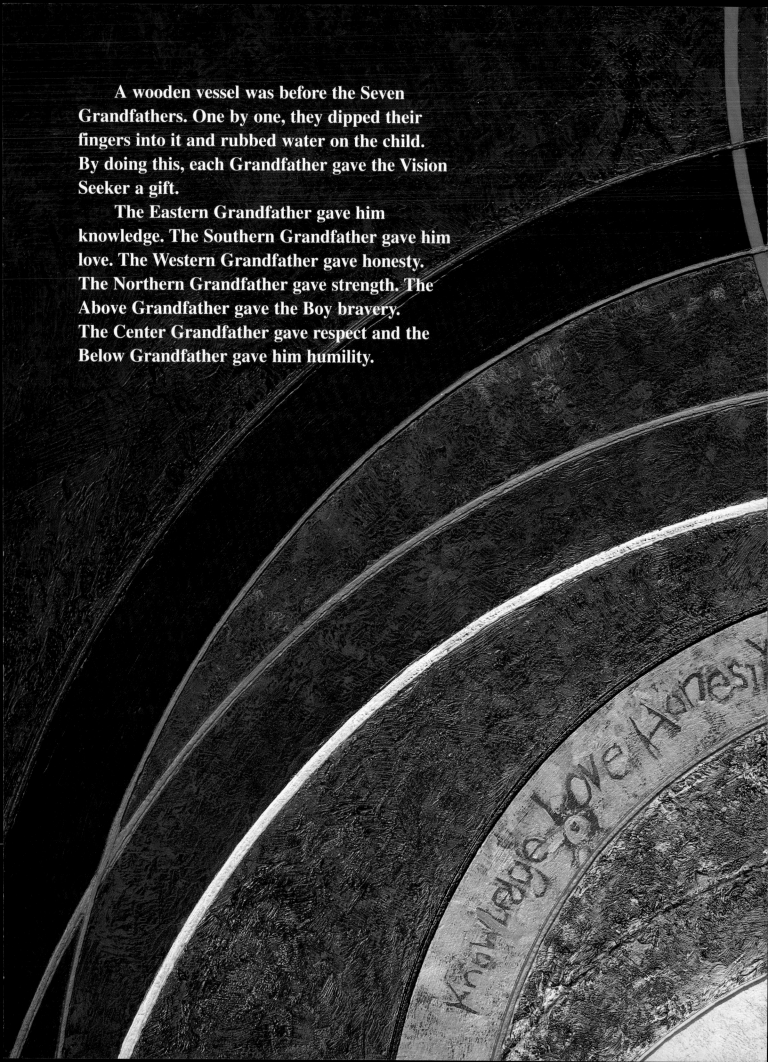

A wooden vessel was before the Seven Grandfathers. One by one, they dipped their fingers into it and rubbed water on the child. By doing this, each Grandfather gave the Vision Seeker a gift.

The Eastern Grandfather gave him knowledge. The Southern Grandfather gave him love. The Western Grandfather gave honesty. The Northern Grandfather gave strength. The Above Grandfather gave the Boy bravery. The Center Grandfather gave respect and the Below Grandfather gave him humility.

Then the Seven Grandfathers instructed the Boy to look into the water in the bottom of the vessel. All of creation was flashing into the Boy's eyes. The sight was so overwhelming that he had to look away. But he had seen enough to receive the sacred instructions. He understood that he must share his vision with his people if they were to survive. The Grandfathers told him it was time to return to the high place.

When the Boy awoke, he was lying, weak and hungry and thirsty, on the ground of the high place. He reached out and picked a little piece of green cedar bough and ate it. With that cedar he broke his fast.

The Boy lay still, trying to remember what he was supposed to do. When he was stronger, he sat up and felt the warmth of sunrise on his back. As he looked down from that high place towards his village, he saw a fire. In the fire he saw the Seven Grandfathers. Then he remembered his vision and the gifts he received from those Grandfathers, the gifts he must share with his people.

The Boy's shadow, cast by the rising sun, fell across the mountain, across the fire, and through the opening on a doorway of a dwelling lodge. And the people waiting there stirred.

The Vision Seeker had come home.

That lodge was built very much like this one. The cedar trail you see there symbolizes the Boy's shadow. The cedar trail leading to the doorway of this Sweat Lodge symbolizes our connection to our past. The cedar road represents our people joining hands back in time to the origins of this teaching. And that mound you see — that crescent-shaped mound with the cedar placed along the top — represents the high place, the place where visions live. The place that is the dark side of the moon.

Miigwetch.

# Author's Note

I am Anishinaabe, one of a nation of people who can trace their past on this land to the beginning of time. We remember our origins in many ways. One way is by using oral teachings as a bridge to our past. *The Vision Seeker* is a teaching of how we received the Sweat Lodge. We use many tools to help us remember, to give us clear images, as we walk the trail back to our beginnings. I can explain it best like this:

The sun is setting in the West. Its warm glow is gradually being replaced by the flickering of firelight. A mound, shaped like a crescent moon, thigh-high in the middle and tapered at the points, faces the fire. A precise line of cedar arcs from point to point along the summit of the mound. At the highest point in the middle of the crescent sits a small, round rock. From that high place, a second precise line of finely-broken cedar needles leads down from the mound towards the centre of the fire. It continues on the other side for another twenty feet to the open, Eastern Doorway of a Sweat Lodge.

From the outside, the Sweat Lodge resembles a canvas-covered dome. This one is approximately eight feet from side to side and about four feet high at the peak of the dome. The sapling frame that supports the canvas can be fashioned from various types of trees, all of which have certain and particular attributes that add to the power and intensity of the Sweat. From the inside, the saplings form a geometric pattern of doorways to each of the four sacred directions. In the ground at the center of the lodge is a circular, shallow pit, twelve inches deep and twenty-four inches across. It is here that the Grandmothers and Grandfathers come to rest, to teach and ultimately to die.

A hissing, snapping sound gathers the minds of a small group of people standing and sitting a short distance from the fire. A young child could smell the tobacco and cedar smoke as it races skyward, forming a long braid, which just as quickly unravels again.

The body holds the cultural memory. It holds the traces of our origins. It is through the practice of the Sweat Lodge that we come back into contact with ourselves. To commemorate requires a ritual act of endurance and purification — a test by fire. The retrieval of images from within the Great Mystery becomes the beacon for unraveling the trail.

To have to flatten some of these images onto paper has been a new challenge for me. I hope I have retained, as much as possible, their holistic qualities and original intent.

*Miigwetch to all Anishinaabeg, the Three Fires Society, Trent University, to all my teachers and Nii Kon Nii Gon Ah.*